For my brother, who has taken care
of me since we were little and still does,
though from a distance.

A.L

LITTLE TIGER
LONDON

CATERPILLAR BOOKS
An imprint of the Little Tiger Group • www.littletiger.co.uk
1 Coda Studios, 189 Munster Road, London SW6 6AW
First published in Great Britain 2020 • Text by Harriet Evans
Text copyright © Caterpillar Books Ltd 2020
Illustrations copyright © Andrés Landazábal 2020
A CIP catalogue record for this book is available
from the British Library
All rights reserved • Printed in China
ISBN: 978-1-84857-946-0
CPB/1400/1343/1219
1 3 5 7 9 10 8 6 4 2

Sisters

Sisters share all your **hopes**,

and they soothe all your **fears**,

As days **drift** to months

and **float** into years.

Your life twists and it turns,
leaps **up** and sinks **down**,

But sisters stay constant
and smooth out your frown.

You'll **wait** and you'll **wonder**
who your sister will be,

And though you may worry,

she'll be **great** – wait and see!

Older sisters might lead
or take a back seat

For each **bold** adventure
and **daring** new feat.

Little sisters may copy

your **style** and your **walk**.

You'll be their **first choice**
when they need to talk.

Friends can become sisters
as you grow up **together**,

Facing dark storms
and enjoying **fair weather**.

Sisters may irritate

and sometimes they're rude,

But on your **worst** days
they'll **brighten** your mood.

Mess somehow just happens
as you both start to **scheme**,

But it turns out alright
when you work as a **team**.

Adventures are better
with a sister or two.

Through **thick** and **thin**,
you make a great crew!

Sisters share all your **hopes**,

and they soothe all your **fears**...

...As days **drift** to months...

...and **float** into years.